With love to Sam and Lydia —S.M.M.

To Tate. Big thanks to Tanner Garlick and Spencer Baird
for their assistance —J.P.

Text copyright © 2019 by Susan McElroy Montanari
Jacket art and interior illustrations copyright © 2019 by Jake Parker
All rights reserved. Published in the United States by Schwartz & Wade Books, an imprint of Random House Children's Books,
a division of Penguin Random House LLC, New York.
Schwartz & Wade Books and the colophon are trademarks of Penguin Random House LLC.
Visit us on the Web! rhcbooks.com
Educators and librarians, for a variety of teaching tools, visit us at RHTeachersLibrarians.com
Library of Congress Cataloging-in-Publication Data is available upon request.
ISBN 978-0-399-55235-9 (hc) — ISBN 978-0-399-55236-6 (lib. bdg.)
ISBN 978-0-399-55237-3 (ebook)
The text of this book is set in Graham.
The illustrations were rendered in ink and colored digitally.
Book design by Rachael Cole
MANUFACTURED IN CHINA
10 9 8 7 6 5 4 3 2 1
First Edition
Random House Children's Books supports the First Amendment and celebrates the right to read.

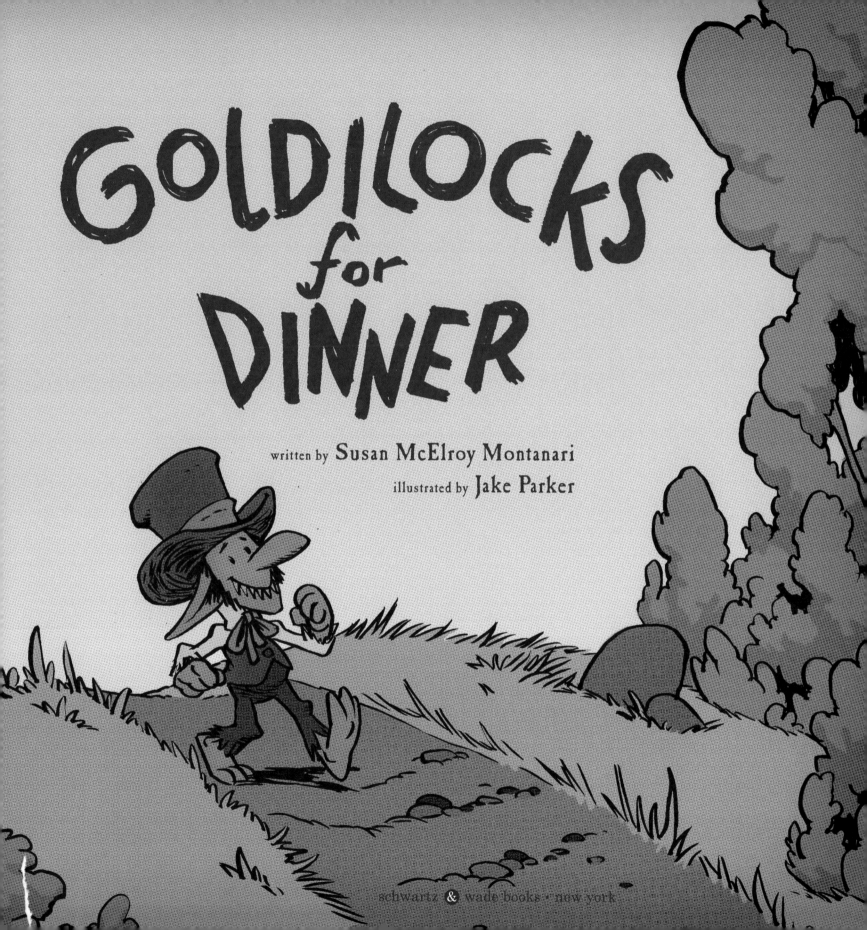

GOLDILOCKS for DINNER

written by **Susan McElroy Montanari**

illustrated by **Jake Parker**

schwartz & wade books · new york

One afternoon as Goblin crossed Troll's bridge, he heard the familiar grumble of his friend.

"Where are you off to?" Troll rumbled, sticking his head out from below.

"To town for a cup of tea. Care to join me?" Goblin asked.

"I'd love to, as long as we don't run into any wretched children."

Goblin nodded in agreement. "Children are gross."

"And smelly—like sugar and spice."

"Yuk! And they're rude!" Goblin's eyes rolled back.

"So rude! That's the worst." Troll shook his head. "There really is no excuse for rudeness."

"I have an idea!" Goblin grinned. "Let's find the rudest child of all and have it for dinner!"

Troll smiled his most fearsome toothy smile and thumped Goblin on the back. "Brilliant, my good fellow, simply brilliant!"

So the two friends started down the road, looking for the rudest child they could find.

They came to a tidy cottage. A little girl stood in front with a watering can. "My, what lovely flowers," Troll said, stopping to admire them.

"They're Mary's," the little girl announced.

"Well, can you please tell Mary she has done an excellent job growing these silver bells," Goblin said.

"No, I don't think I will," the girl answered. "Tell her yourself."

"We'd be happy to," Troll replied, looking around.

"So go ahead. I'm Mary." The girl pointed a thumb at herself.

"Ah! Then I suppose we already have," said Goblin.

Goblin turned to his friend. "She is quite rude," he whispered.

"Hmmm," Troll whispered back. "I would say she is more contrary than rude."

"If you say so," Goblin replied, tipping his hat to Mary. "Let's carry on."

As they passed Simple Simon's Bakery, Troll pointed. "See there, that boy has stuck his thumb in a pie and pulled out a plum. How rude!"

"Well, that would depend on whether he has purchased the pie already," Goblin replied. "If so, it may just be disgusting."

Just then, another cottage door slammed and three
bears came out waving their paws and talking loudly.

"What's going on?" Goblin asked.

"She's in there—sleeping!" the biggest bear said.

"Who?" Troll asked.

"We don't know," his wife said.

"We came home and found her curled
up in our little one's bed."

"She just came over uninvited and let herself into your house?" Goblin asked.

"That's not all," the big bear answered, shaking his head.

The littlest bear sniffled. "She ate our porridge and broke my chair."

"*And* she snores," his mother added.

Goblin shook his head. "Letting oneself into someone's house, eating their food, breaking their furniture—"

"And snoring!" Troll added.

"I believe we've found our winner!" Goblin declared.

The girl poked her head out the window. "What do you mean, 'winner'? What did I win?"

Troll turned to Goblin. "Eavesdropping, too," he whispered.

"What did I win?" the girl demanded, jumping out the window.

Goblin smiled, showing all one hundred and fifty-two of his glittery teeth. "You have won a very special, very surprising prize. Come to my cottage tonight at six and we will give it to you." He handed the girl a card. "Here's the address. And don't be late."

"Yes, it would be rude to be late." Troll stifled a giggle.

"I'll be there," the girl said, grabbing the card and running away.

Troll and Goblin said good-bye to the bears and hurried off to make preparations.

At Goblin's, Troll set the table while Goblin stirred a huge cauldron over the fire.

When the girl arrived at six-fifteen, Goblin clapped his hands and Troll grinned as they both rushed to the door.

"Where's my prize?" the girl demanded, standing at the door tapping her foot.

Goblin smiled. "We declare you to be the rudest child of all. And to teach you a lesson, we've decided—"

"—to have you for dinner and—" Troll interrupted.

"Aaaah!" The girl screamed a horrified scream,
then turned and ran away as fast as she could.

"That was rude," Troll observed.

"Well, what did we expect?" Goblin agreed.

"We invited her over and made this wonderful meal, just so we could teach her some table manners."

Goblin shut the door. "Learning good table manners is the key to proper behavior."

"What shall we do now?" asked Troll.

"We shall sit down and enjoy our dinner," Goblin replied.

"I will remove her place setting," said Troll.

And that is what the two friends did.